MR. HAPPY

by Roger Hargreaves

PSS!

PRICE STERN SLOAN

An Imprint of Penguin Group (USA) Inc.

On the other side of the world, where the sun shines hotter than here, and where the trees are a hundred feet tall, there is a country called Happyland.

As you might very well expect, everybody who lives in Happyland is as happy as the day is long. Wherever you go, you see smiling faces all around. It's such a happy place that even the flowers seem to smile in Happyland.

All the animals in Happyland are happy as well.

If you've never seen a smiling mouse, or a happy cat or dog, or even a smiling worm—go to Happyland.

This is a story about someone who lived in Happyland, who happened to be called Mr. Happy.

Mr. Happy was fat, and round, and happy!

He lived in a small cottage, beside a lake, at the foot of a mountain, and close to the woods.

One day, while Mr. Happy was walking in those woods near his home, he came across something which was really very exciting.

There in the trunk of one of the very tall trees was a door. Not a very large door, but it was certainly a door. A small, narrow, yellow door.

Definitely a door!

"I wonder who lives there?" thought Mr. Happy, and he turned the handle of that small, narrow, yellow door.

The door wasn't locked and it swung open quite easily.

Just inside the small, narrow, yellow door was a small, narrow, winding staircase, leading down.

Mr. Happy squeezed his rather large body through the rather thin doorway and began to walk down the stairs.

The stairs went 'round and 'round and down and down and 'round and down and down and 'round.

Finally, after a long time, Mr. Happy reached the bottom of the staircase.

He looked around and saw in front of him another small, narrow door. But this one was red.

Mr. Happy knocked on the door.

"Who's there?" said a voice. It was a sad, squeaky sort of voice. "Who's there?"

Mr. Happy slowly pushed open the red door. There, sitting on a stool, was somebody who looked exactly like Mr. Happy, except that he didn't look happy at all.

In fact, he looked downright miserable.

"Hello," said Mr. Happy. "I'm Mr. Happy."

"Oh, are you really," sniffed the person who looked like Mr. Happy but wasn't. "Well, my name is Mr. Miserable, and I'm the most miserable person in the world."

"Why are you so miserable?" asked Mr. Happy.

"Because I am," replied Mr. Miserable.

Mr. Miserable hesitated, and then followed.

Up and up the winding staircase they went. Up and up and 'round and 'round and up and 'round and 'round and up until they came out into the woods.

"Follow me," said Mr. Happy again, and they both walked through the woods back to Mr. Happy's cottage.

Mr. Miserable stayed in Mr. Happy's cottage for quite a while. And during that time, the most remarkable thing happened.

Because he was living in Happyland, Mr. Miserable very, very slowly stopped being miserable and started to be happy.

His mouth stopped turning down at the corners.

And very, very slowly, it started turning up at the corners.

And eventually, Mr. Miserable did something that he'd never done in his whole life . . .

He smiled!

And then he chuckled, which turned into a giggle, which became a laugh. A big, booming, hearty, huge, giant, large, enormous laugh.

And Mr. Happy was so surprised that he started to laugh as well. And both of them laughed and laughed.

They laughed until their sides hurt and their eyes watered.

Mr. Miserable and Mr. Happy laughed and laughed and laughed and laughed.

They went outside and still they laughed.

And because they were laughing so much, everybody who saw them started laughing as well. Even the birds in the trees started to laugh at the thought of somebody called Mr. Miserable who just couldn't stop laughing.

And that's really the end of the story, except to say that if you ever feel as miserable as Mr. Miserable used to, you know exactly what to do, don't you?

Just turn your mouth up at the corners.

Go on!